THE PLANTING OF BÔ-KEDÉN

THE PLANTING
OF BÔ-KEDÉN

Based on the
Carew Manuscript 131
"Manuscriptus Caelani"
attributed to
the
Writer of Calan

✠✠✠

Freely translated into English
by
John Kincheloe

SPIRIT LINES PRESS

THE PLANTING OF BÔ-KEDÉN
© John Kincheloe, 2021

Printed in the United States of America

First Printing 2021

ISBN 978-0-9831177-3-5

Spirit Lines Press
P.O. Box 1240
Alcalde, NM 87511

Set in Perpetua and High Tower fonts with Felix Titling

The book design was inspired by Liam Miller's Dolmen Press edition of
THE TAIN, translated by Thomas Kinsella.

Cover design and concept development by
Jacob Daroca-Kincheloe

Book design by
John Kincheloe

Book layout by
Tracy Atkins - The BookMakers.com

For Daniel

"Child, if you will, it is mythology. It is but truth, not fact: an image, not the very real. But then it is My mythology.... this is My inventing, this is the veil under which I have chosen to appear even from the first until now. For this end I made your senses and for this end your imagination, that you might see My face and live. What would you have?"

C.S. Lewis, *Pilgrim's Regress*

THE FIRST PART

HIS WOUND no longer hurt. It would heal, he knew. Rakedén knew many things with clarity now, as he walked ahead to battle. The feeding crows and jackdaws scattered as he crossed the bloody ground and stepped across the fallen men. Some of these were enemies, some had been his friends. Now lying in the war-scorched field, they were all the same. This was not the time for pain, not the day for grief.

For he saw his enemy approaching, sword flashing as he came. Rakedén could see the coming struggle. He saw the hungry sword come at him, and the staff that sent a helmet singing into sky. And more he saw. A son. A friend. The enemy drew nearer. And Rakedén would see a white and shining hill. As the rattle of the armor came closer, he could only hear a distant solemn song that focused his attention. In that time, outside of time, he knew more than he could know. He saw the tree. He saw a seed. And he was smiling when the blade first rang against his stout wooden staff.

So the story is begun.

THE SECOND PART

A HUSH hung over the fine old house of Rakedén. Visitors stood quietly before the large fireplace, gazing into the heap of fading embers. There were others who walked slowly through the rooms, speaking in whispers with close friends. Even in the great room so used to feasts and merriment, there was now only quiet. A serious mood had fallen over the whole place, for the master of the house, the wise and good Rakedén, lay upon his bed near to death.

Not only in this house but throughout the whole city of Nebis the people awaited some word concerning Rakedén. Wealthy and poor alike were deeply saddened by his low condition, and they hoped for some miracle to restore Rakedén to his former strength.

But Rakedén, himself, knew his time had come. So he sent for his son, Baloe, who was still a boy. The old man called him to his bedside and with a weakened voice spoke with him.

"Come near and listen." He gestured to Baloe with a thin hand.

The boy leaned closer, and gently put his hand on his father's arm. Afternoon sunlight from the window fell across the boy, and Rakedén was silent for a time as he studied the young face as if to read its secret, its deepest thought and feeling.

The old man's expression turned slowly to a smile as he remembered many things, and as he saw what would surely come. At last he understood. And in that moment of inner vision, he saw a glimpse of his place in the Great Pattern of all that is and sensed the future that would call forth his son. Rakedén closed his eyes, and he spoke to Baloe.

"I have lived a good life and have made a good life for my family. I am proud of this. I have lived according to the Way of Bô-Kedén, the true way of a human being." He reached across the side of his bed and placed his hand on Baloe's shoulder. "I have been given a fine son who is strong. You have learned much of Bô-Kedén. You know the *Sayings* of the Powerful One and sing the *Canticles* well. You make this weak heart sing with pride."

The old man paused then began to speak again. "Baloe, my son—my only son—now that my time has come to die...."

"No, Father!" Baloe cried out, as he fell to his knees beside the bed. "*Arbolas vibayos!* You will not die...." And he tried his best to hold his father.

"Come, come," Rakedén said in a thin voice, but in his fatherly way. "I do not fear my death, and neither should you fear it. Winter comes, and the tree must lose its leaves. But remember the word of Allwise Bô-Kedén:

> Bare be his branches,
> They rattle with Death.
> Yet leaves in spring
> Will push aside the snow.
> We sing of Life,
> We hold the branches green.
> Death again is fooled.

He held his son's shoulder tight. "My time has come, Baloe. But there are truths of Bô-Kedén that you must be shown before I leave you."

Baloe turned his head and looked into his father's eyes, "Truths to be shown, Father? What truths?"

"The truths of the Planting of Bô-Kedén," his father replied calmly.

But Baloe still did not understand, and he told his father so.

The boy straightened himself and wiped the tears from his eyes with the sleeve of his shirt. Rakedén took his son's hand and held it firmly in his own. He spoke softly, "Baloe, you are young, but you will soon have great understanding. The one who will teach you is an old one named Mekloth. You have heard his name before. He lives alone in the high Calanites, on a ridge near Na-Groud, the place of Dark Trees."

4

"Na-Groud —"

The boy said nothing more. The mention of the place of the Dark Trees had conjured up a strangeness that, for a moment, took away his tears. All who lived in Nebis knew that Na-Groud was a place to be avoided. Shadows were said to be alive in that place.

"Yes, Baloe, you must go there. It is important for our family and for Nebis. Do not listen to your fears, my son. Forget for now what you have heard of Na-Groud. The Almighty One will protect you as you travel. Go there and find my old friend Mekloth. Tell him this—tell him '*Kaeres es.*' It is the time." He paused, and then looked at his son's face, still awash in the bright light of the late afternoon. "It is time to plant the Bô-Kedén."

So it was that young Baloe, his eyes still burning with sadness, set off up the mountain in search of Mekloth.

-ABELA-

THE THIRD PART

THE ROUGH TRAIL from Nebis to the place of Dark Trees was not an easy way even in summer. The old travelers had a name for the stony path. They called it "The Foot Eater." Baloe's way was made more difficult still by winter storms that had heaped ice on the mountain. The trail was often filled with drifting snow and, at times, could not be found at all. But the boy knew the importance of his task, and he would not be discouraged by the sharp stones and biting cold that gnawed at his feet. At every turn and steep rise the way was treacherous with rock and ice, but when the journey would seem too difficult, Baloe always returned to his father's words. Almighty Bô-Kedén would see him safely to the place where Mekloth lived.

At last the mountain path began to level off, and Baloe realized he was near the place. As the way opened into a clearing, he could see far down into the valley where his tiny village lay like the toy houses his father had made for him. He had never before traveled so high up the mountain. Hawks soared past in the clouded sky below him, like feathers in wind.

"You are quite young to come to Na-Groud, Traveler. This is the place of Dark Trees."

Baloe spun about and nearly fell, startled by the one who had spoken to him. Up the mountain he saw a man standing atop a great jagged rock. He wore a loose brown robe—or was it black? In his fist he held a tall staff. The stranger's long beard lashed out suddenly in a gust that shook ice from the branches all around. The man's rough cloak whipped to one side sharply in the wind.

7

Baloe stepped back. "I—I am Baloe," the boy began, "Son of Rakedén, from the town of Nebis. I have been sent here by my father to find one called Mekloth. Do you know this man or where I might find him?"

The man above stood silent awhile, his piercing eyes fixed upon the boy. Then as suddenly as he had spoken, he turned and was gone from atop the broken rock.

Now for the first time on his journey up the mountain, Baloe felt real fear. Who could this have been? A living shadow from the place of Dark Trees? An enemy of Bô-Kedén? Would this sorcerer send sharp rocks down upon him and prevent the journey to Mekloth? Questions and doubts filled the boy's head, and every rattling branch and fluttering leaf renewed his terror.

In his fear, though, Baloe went again to the words his father had given him. Bô-Kedén, the All Powerful Bô-Kedén, was with him on this journey. He was not alone at Na-Groud. Once again, he found strength and his resolve. He knew he must find Mekloth to give him the message. So Baloe looked about, then once more started up the mountain.

Before the boy had moved two paces up the trail, however, the robed stranger appeared again. This time he stood directly in the boy's path. Baloe took an uneasy breath and spoke to the one before him, "I must be on my way to find the one called Mekloth."

The stranger lifted his tall staff slowly, and then said, "You need travel no farther, young Baloe, for I am the one you seek. *Mekloth ek baen*" (which in the old language means, "I am Mekloth").

The bearded man walked slowly toward Baloe, studying the boy's face. He stopped close to the boy and planted the end of his staff into the ground. Then he spoke with a full and welcoming voice, "Baloe, Son of Rakedén from Nebis. Yes...yes —"

The Bearded One smiled broadly and continued as he clapped his hand onto the boy's shoulder. "Well, my young friend, what is the reason for your long journey to me at such a delightful time of year?" Another strong gust of wind sent snow and fallen leaves into a swirl about their feet.

Baloe steadied himself and replied to the Old One's question. "My father is ill, and though I do not know why, he has sent me to you. He told me to tell you this. He said, 'Tell Mekloth: *Kaeres es*. It is time to plant the Bô-Kedén.' I do not understand this, and I do not know why I should tell it to you. Except that it was my father's wish that I come and speak his words." The boy had told this quickly, but then he halted. Distracted, he looked down into the valley, toward Nebis. He turned back to face Mekloth. "I think I should return to him now. Rakedén, my father, is dying."

Mekloth looked into Baloe's eyes and saw the deep sadness. The Old One raised his staff in a way that was both strong and wise. He quietly spoke, "Yes, you should go back to your father. But before you return, I must tell you why your father sent you to me."

"Then please tell me quickly, for I must soon be on my way home."

"You must know, young Baloe, that your father sent you here for a purpose greater than you know. Do not be anxious about the time. Rakedén will not let go of his life until you have returned. Come walk with me. Listen to what I tell you. This is your father's wish."

The two began walking slowly on a path that led to a rocky place above them, and Mekloth began:

"Many years ago, before your eyes opened to this world, a terrible war raged across the Plains of Calan. Invaders from the north devastated our land and enslaved many of our people. You have not heard the name Tzokan before. Long Scar he is called. It was he who led the invaders against us. Tzokan's greed for power and wealth brought destruction even to your little town of Nebis. You have seen the ruins there, Baloe?"

"I have," the boy replied, "but no one would speak of them."

"This is so. And it is good that you not know until now. But now is the time for you to hear of the battle of Nebishan. Know this, Son of Rakedén: the people of the Calan Plains have always been a peaceful people, lovers of verse and music. From the beginning we have lived according to the Wisdom of the Tree, for it is through Tree Bô-Kedén that we are strong as well as wise. As it is said,

The way of Bô-Kedén is peace,
The oak boasts not its strength.
Who shall fell the one wise in the Way,
And who shall prevail against him?

"And know this. Long Scar came to take this peace from us. His way was dark, and he used his power to bring misery to Calan. He stole our food and murdered our people. He mocked the Way of Bô-Kedén.

"The Plains people were not warlike, but we rose up against the forces of Tzokan. At first there were defeats for us, but then followed small victories. Success came to us not through our own efforts, but through the power of Bô-Kedén. We were wise not to confuse our own power with His. We were led into battle by four warriors whose strength and wisdom were only surpassed by their trust in Lord Bô-Kedén.

"It was finally at Nebis that the defenders of Calan stood against the full army of Tzokan. The battle raged for days, Baloe. Many were killed on both sides. Death was the only victor on those days.

"As night began to fall on the final day of the conflict, the battle horns of Tzokan sounded, and the Northern warriors disengaged the fight. All retreated to their positions. Then across the battle plain, strewn with fallen weapons and fallen soldiers, a riderless black horse raced at full gallop from the invader's camp to the front lines of our armies. Lashed to its rein was a message—a challenge from Tzokan himself to decide the outcome of the battle through single-handed combat with our leader. The loser's armies would accept defeat and surrender.

"As darkness fell, the Four Leaders together decided that the bloodshed of common battle must end, and they were confident that the power of Bô-Kedén would bring victory. It was decided by the Four that one of them would fight Tzokan. And the one who stepped forward, Baloe, Son of Rakedén, was your father."

"Father?" the boy said as he started at this revelation.

"Yes, Baloe, on the following day it was your father alone who met Tzokan the Invader in battle at Nebishan. It was Rakedén who cast aside his sword in the presence of Tzokan and picked up a wooden staff like this one to do battle with the evil one. Long Scar earned his name in that struggle with your father. It was Rakedén who overcame death on that final day.

But Baloe's head was full of questions. "Why was I never told this before, and why do you tell me now?"

"It was the wisdom of the Four to know that the same pride and violence of Tzokan should not be continued through the telling of stories of human boldness and power. The defenders chose to be silent about Tzokan, about the war, and even about the great battle of Nebishan. It was their way of affirming the sacred power of Bô-Kedén and the way of peace. The Four chose even no longer to be leaders. Your father left a position of high honor to become a planter and to help rebuild Nebis."

"And you, Mekloth? Were you one of the Four?"

"Yes," the older one replied and then paused as memories filled his eyes. "Yes, Baloe. In that time I was one of the Four. And after Nebishan I came alone to this place. To the edge of Na-Groud, this place of fears and dark trees —" He gestured to the forest uphill from them, "To understand the way of Bô-Kedén. To face my fears. To forget the bloody war we fought. To find meaning again, and peace."

Baloe listened intently as Mekloth continued.

"The other two of us traveled to the west. Lerin of Baolind and Timoth, Son of Kell.

"And now I tell you this because your father knows he is dying, and his power must become yours. You must soon begin learning the mysteries of Tree Bô-Kedén. *Kaeres es*. It is the time."

Baloe's words came quickly, "I can't begin to understand all of this—the mysteries of Bô-Kedén? Is there more to learn than the *Canticles* and the *Sayings*? *Kaeres es?*"

"You have only begun to know the power. Come quickly with me. Before you leave you must begin to learn the meaning of the Planting."

The Old One turned and climbed nimbly, effortlessly up the rough rock path. Baloe followed.

A short distance up the hill they came to a ledge that bordered a forest of immense hardwood trees. The forest appeared to cover the entire top of the rise above them. Its dense foliage shaded the forest floor from sunlight to such an extent that it seemed blackened by soot only a few feet into the woods. Baloe stiffened at the realization that this was Na-Groud itself, the place of Dark Trees, the place of Strangeness.

The sound of liquid pouring brought his attention back to the present moment. He looked and saw Mekloth emptying something from a cask into a wooden cup. As the boy drew nearer, Mekloth stood up before him and held out the cup. Baloe reached to take it and glanced into Mekloth's eyes. They were intensely blue, gleaming with wisdom.

Then Mekloth spoke. "You must drink this now. This is your first taste of the power of Bô-Kedén. Do not be afraid. Drink of the Wisdom of the Tree," and he nodded.

Baloe raised the cup and looked into the reddish-brown liquid as he drank. Its resinous taste was at first bitter then it was sweet. He swallowed and it warmed his throat. Again he swallowed, and the cup was empty. Immediately a feeling of fullness came to his head, and he realized Mekloth was speaking to him.

"Close your eyes, Baloe. Close your eyes. Yes."

Baloe did so and took a deep breath.

Mekloth continued, "Now turn and look at what is behind you. Tell me what you see."

Baloe opened his eyes and blinked heavily. Then he turned from the darkness of the forest toward the open sky and the burning sun behind him. The golden light was overwhelming. He squinted his eyes tightly, and with his hands he shielded them from the splintering brightness.

"What do you see on the edge of the cliff before you?" Mekloth quietly asked.

"I—I see a dead tree—a gnarled, dead tree," the boy said, still shielding his eyes.

"Very well. Now close your eyes again. Yes. And now open them and tell me what you see."

"The tree—it is alive! That tree is all green now —" In a boy's astonishment he threw his arms into the air, spreading his hands to the sky, "The tree has come alive!"

"Yes, Baloe. Now once more, close your eyes. Open them again and look to the tree."

"The tree—is gone. Mekloth, there is no tree there... Master, where did it go? This is strange. Tell me how it was there and now...." He held out an empty hand toward the barren cliff before him.

"The tree is still there, Baloe," Mekloth spoke as he led the boy through snow and leaves to the place where the tree had been. "You will learn to see soon enough. As for now," he said, kneeling down and reaching to the icy ground, "You must take these with you and return to your father."

Mekloth picked up three rounded brown seeds from the cold earth. He stood up and placed them in the boy's hand.

"Take care with these," he spoke. "One you will give to your father as he asks you. You will understand later what to do with the other two. Now be off to your good father. Your feet be sure and your eyes keen. Bô-Kedén be with you."

"And here —" Mekloth said as he took a small cloth sack from his cloak and handed it to the boy. "Here is some bread for your journey home. Farewell, my new friend."

So it was that Baloe set off down the mountain to return to his father.

-ABELA-

THE FOURTH PART

ON HIS ICY WAY Baloe walked. Then part-way down the mountain he saw a feeble old man in the distance, tottering down the difficult path in front of him. Glad to find another person on the trail, Baloe ran up closer to the fellow and called out, "Old Man, we should walk along together. Share this loaf of bread with me."

"Old? Old, did you say?" the bent-over figure cackled as he made an effort to turn toward the boy.

"Yes, for I see your back is stooped with age and the years have whitened your whiskers. I am sorry if I —"

But the Bent One interrupted, "Would I be young then if my back were straight, and my hair were black? If I appeared young would I then be young? Answer? The answer now, Boy?"

"My answer must be no," Baloe responded with amusement as the two continued down the path. "So, correct me, Sir, if you will. How old would you be?"

"Young as my tongue and older than my teeth," was the old one's quick reply.

"If that is your age, my new old friend," the boy answered back with a laugh, "then I am the same age as you. For I, too, am young as my tongue and older than my teeth. But allow me to say I think your tongue is wiser than mine."

"Yes," said the Bent One, "for I know my age and you do not. In that measure, at least, I am wiser than the Boy. But I will find out how much wiser I am." He held up an old walking stick bent crooked as he was, and at the same time blurted out, "I have a crusty riddle for the Young One! Ha! What is heavy as stone but light as a feather? What is it, now?"

"An easy one," the boy answered straight away. "And we are walking through the answer: it is snow. It falls through the air light as bird feathers, but on the ground it is heavy and difficult to shovel from the paths. My father told me that one before my sister was born. That is how I know my answer is the right one."

Baloe stopped walking for a moment and thought. Then at once he said, "Now I have one for you, my friend—another one my father told me:

> I am brown and full of sound
> When I sleep upon the ground.
> I am amber and I'm green
> And sometimes nothing seen.

The Bent One crossed his hands over the end of his walking stick, and he considered it a while. Then he let out a wren-like chuckle and said, "I'm not brown, but I am full of sound when I sleep upon the ground. They say I snore, but how would I know? I'm asleep when I do it." Then he snorted like a snoring hog and laughed.

"But let's see now." He stretched out a bony hand and seemed to write some words in the air with his finger. Then at once he stopped. "I have it. I have it! Leaves it is! Amber in the fall and green in summer. And in fall they lie down brown and they talk when you walk upon 'em. Crunch, crunch. In winter the trees are bald as I might be—no leaves, so nothing seen. So...leaves it is. Leaves!" And he let out a rude triumphant hoot.

Then abruptly he tapped his bent stick on the icy ground three times. "Now my turn again. Who is this?

> Strong and rough, he never sleeps,
> But cut him and he weeps.
> His finger holds a rook.
> He is the finest cook.
> Tell me of the name he keeps.

The Bent One tugged down on the wide hood of his cloak, and said with his creaky laugh, "Tell me who he is."

Baloe repeated the riddle and turned it around in his mind. "Hmmm. Bird on his finger. He cooks and never sleeps...."

The Bent One blurted out, "Cooks and never sleeps! Yes! Now tell me who he is. Tell me who he is...." And he laughed a wheezy laugh.

Then all at once Baloe knew it. "A tree it is! Tree is the name he keeps. Strong and rough, the rook sits on his branch. His bark weeps sap if it's been cut. And wood cooks our food. A tree it is. A tree is who he is." And it was Baloe's turn to laugh loud.

"Your answer is correct," the Bent One spoke, his voice creaking like an ancient door opening. "You can be wise because of certain things you know. But I say also you can be wise in not knowing. Listen: you cannot know why you awaken in the mornings as you do. You do not awaken yourself. You are asleep! Some days a noise will cause you to open your eyes. But other days you stay asleep and you dream through the greatest commotion. And why is this? That is the riddle, and no one can know it. In sleep you are like the seed that falls to the earth, dead and dry, only to sprout suddenly to life. The seed does not know why it comes to life, but each spring it rejoices that it lives. You cannot know why you awaken, Boy, and neither can I. We do not have this knowledge. Like the seed we only have rejoicing. You are wise to know that," and the Bent One tilted his crooked staff toward the boy, "Wise in not knowing."

Baloe was then nearly lost in his thoughts and could only say, "You are much wiser than I, this much I do know."

The Bent One replied, "Do not think you lack wisdom, Boy. Truest wisdom comes first from the heart, then from experience of years. So it is with the tree, as you must know. The strength is in the center. The hollow tree will fall."

At those words Baloe stopped and faced his old companion who was hunched over and leaning on his crooked stick. The strange events of the journey grew like thick vines together in his memory: his father's request, the icy way to Na-Groud, his finding of Mekloth, the story of the Battle of

Nebishan, the vision of the trees and the seeds. The wind died down as Baloe looked at the feeble old man before him and as he recalled his words.

And all on the mountain fell silent as he then realized.

Like some great plant rising toward the light, the old man straightened and stood tall. And throwing back the hood of his coat, he said in a full and familiar voice, "You are right, my young friend. *Mekloth ek baen*. And now I know that you are indeed Baloe, son of Rakedén. There is much we have to talk about as we walk to see your good father."

So down the icy mountain they continued the journey, Baloe and Mekloth. Sharing a loaf of bread, the two talked of life and of the wisdom and power of Bô-Kedén. They spoke of appearances and of what is real. And they made their way to Nebis in the valley below, and to the house of Rakedén.

-ABELA-

THE FIFTH PART

RAKEDÉN opened his eyes as Baloe and Mekloth entered the room. He held out his hand as Baloe came to his side. "You have done well, my son. And I am sure you have learned much from my old wise friend. Mekloth, how have you been?"

Mekloth drew near to the bed as he spoke. "The winters are growing colder for me, but I have been well. Lord Bô-Kedén provides much for me on the mountain."

"He has provided Nebis with much as well," Rakedén replied. "The town has grown and there is much that is new. But it is still a town that lives for its people. Would that I had more time to show you about your old Nebis."

"Is there much time?" Mekloth asked as he placed his hand on Baloe's shoulder.

Rakedén shook his head as he looked into Mekloth's eyes. "We must begin tonight."

And so through the night the three talked. Baloe was told many things of Bô-Kedén and of the Planting. There was no time for sorrow, for there was much to be done.

The following morning Rakedén called to be taken to his chosen place in the forest, as was their custom. All in the city followed behind, and there were many tears for Rakedén.

When they arrived at the place, Rakedén called for his wife and family. One by one they came, and then it was time for Baloe to speak with his father. Blinking back tears he moved to Rakedén's side and looked down upon his father.

Rakedén spoke to him: "Baloe, we have talked of my death before. That does not keep us from being sad now as we speak."

There were tears in the old man's eyes as he continued. "Be good to your mother and your sisters. Care for them, Baloe. Tend to them. They are your branches. But always first do the Will of Lord Bô-Kedén. Their protection will come from this. Remember, my son.

"Mekloth will guide you, but above all Bô-Kedén himself will guide you if you seek to know his Way. His is the Way of all life."

"I will remember, Father."

"I know that you will."

Rakedén looked above him as he lay. The sky was clear and bright, and the birds chattered in the great bare branches above as again he spoke: "Baloe, it is time."

Baloe took from his belt a pouch, and opening it, he took from it one of the three seeds Mekloth had given him on the mountain. He placed the seed in his father's open hand and stepped away as Rakedén spoke in a voice both frail and full of strength: "Out of the wisdom of Bô-Kedén did I grow, and so will his wisdom grow from me. I plant the Bô-Kedén."

And Rakedén opened his mouth and, placing the seed in it, closed his eyes to the world.

-ABELA-

THE SIXTH PART

WEEKS PASSED and months until winter had had its say. The sadness of Rakedén's passing would remain with the people of Nebis for years, but the joy of the new spring lightened their hearts, and Bô-Kedén again showed them the power of life.

It was then that the sprout appeared over the grave of Rakedén.

Now Baloe had been told it would come. He remembered the words Mekloth spoke before he returned to the mountain: "Out of your father's wisdom will grow the true wisdom of Bô-Kedén. And it shall become yours, as it was your father's. You shall take it and make of it your staff."

So it did happen. So did the seedling begin from out of the father's wisdom. It grew slender and strong out of the place where Rakedén lay, and all the people of Nebis marveled at it.

Baloe watched over the young tree as it grew. He continued to learn the Way of Bô-Kedén and to grow in the Lord's own wisdom.

So it happened also that after three years had passed, Baloe went to the place in the forest, and he took the new tree and fashioned from its wood a staff.

Then it was that Baloe set his face toward the mountain, and with his wooden staff in hand he made his way to Mekloth.

-THA ABELA MAKLOHT-

THE SEVENTH PART

THE OLD ONE rejoiced to see Baloe traveling along the path below. Mekloth ran to greet his visitor with a hearty embrace, and the two began walking up the final rise together.

Baloe spoke as they climbed the path, "It was as you said, Teacher. The seed was well planted, and Bô-Kedén did grow. And as we climb, I carry his wisdom on the mountain. In my hand I hold the Lord's staff, and I am humble beside it."

Mekloth nodded slowly then spoke. "You carry his wisdom well, Son of Rakedén, for you do not confuse the Lord's Wisdom with your own. That is always the danger. One must be ever humble before the wisdom of Tree Bô-Kedén. It pleases me that you have come to know this so soon."

"But there is yet much I must learn," Baloe replied. "I have come to you seeking to know the Way of Bô-Kedén."

"Then first know this, Baloe. The Way of Lord Bô-Kedén is known in the heart. This I cannot teach you. I can only show you how I have come to see his power, wisdom, and love. It will be in your own heart that the Lord will finally make his Way known to you.

"But yes, I will tell you how I see the Way of Bô-Kedén. Follow me now."

Mekloth turned off the path and led Baloe through the forest. After a short distance, Mekloth pointed up the mountain to a long rounded hut. It was made of bent saplings, thatch and vine. The neatly framed door seemed made of sticks woven tightly over each other.

"It is not the fine house of Rakedén, but it is all that I need," Mekloth said as he swung back the door and entered. Baloe followed him in.

The old man picked up a flickering lamp and lit several others. Then Baloe could see about the place. There were benches and a table of rough wood before them. As they walked to the far end of the hut, light fell on some baskets of fruits and nuts. And past these the boy brushed by fragrant herbs of all sorts drying on the walls.

Then Mekloth stopped before a small fireplace and lifted his lamp, lighting still another which hung from the ridgepole above them. The wick sputtered then burned brightly, casting light all about the end of the hut. It was only then that Baloe looked to the wall above the fireplace. There in the lamplight he saw a great round slab of wood suspended from the roof by two ropes bound about its edge.

The old man spoke as Baloe gazed up at the round of wood, "You must begin to know the Center.

"Before us hangs a piece of wood, cross-cut from the trunk of an ancient oak. You see the rings of many years of growth. Here there was a fire. And here a very dry spring," he gestured. "And the year after, Bô-Kedén sent his blessing to the tree, you see? The wood itself speaks the story of its life, with all truth.

"But Baloe, this is not only a cut through the trunk of a tree—a slab that tells the story of its own life of many years. This wood carries another kind of truth. For what is before us is an image of the Center.

"Year upon year the growth of the tree makes circles around its center. But the center remains the same, ever giving rise to new growth. The center lies deep within the life of the tree, but it is much smaller, you see, than what is grown. Follow the rings, smaller and smaller to the center. And smaller still, to the tiniest point. And within the heart of that lies the Center: the source of life, power, and wisdom."

But Baloe was puzzled. He turned toward Mekloth, saying, "Master, I have come to learn the Way of Bô-Kedén, to learn of power. But you tell me of the center of a tree. You speak of power but teach me only about something small."

"Does it surprise you that I speak of smallness?" Mekloth then asked the boy. "Are you surprised, as well, that a plant begins as a seed—that the tree whose mighty roots have split the stones in its way begins as a windblown seed?

Listen: within each seed lies the Center, as well. A plant will grow from seed—first a tiny shoot, then the small stalk with leaves, then a young plant. Ever upward, ever outward it grows, above and below the ground. But understand this: the power continues to lie in the smallness of the Center. This is the source of its strength. It is the source of all strength."

Baloe then gestured to the round of wood, saying, "But Mekloth, doesn't the Center grow through the length of the tree? As the plant grows tall, does not its center grow with it—even as the tree before us once grew?"

And Mekloth replied. "We stand before an image of the Center, but we must not confuse the image with the reality. The Center is the source of the growing, but it does not grow. It has no need of being larger. If such power can be contained within a single seed, why would this power need to grow? In the Center there is all power, and nothing can become greater."

"Then where is the center of the tree?" Baloe asked, still not understanding.

"The true Center lies within the life of the tree. It is not in the strongest limb; it is not in the deepest root or in the stoutest trunk. The parts of the tree—wood, bark, leaves—these grow out of the Center, but they are not the Center. The power of Bô-Kedén creates the mighty tree and the beautiful flower, but trunk and blossom are only signs of that power and not the power itself. So it is with the Center, and so it is sung:

> Within the tree but not the tree,
> Changing all but yet unchanging,
> Great always but ever small.

Baloe stood in silence before the round of wood, thinking on the words Mekloth spoke. Then all at once he realized what the Old One had shown him when they had first met. First there was the dead tree, old, gnarled and bent, then a strong tree, green with foliage, and finally there was no tree at all, only three seeds. But had he not been shown that the Center was present in all that he saw there? Was not the same Center present in life and in death, in beginning and end? And beyond this, what else could the Center be than the very dwelling place of Bô-Kedén. Is not the hidden presence of the Lord the true life of the tree, the true reality?

Then Mekloth, who knew what young Baloe was thinking, spoke, "Yes, now you understand the vision. You have learned to see. You have begun to know the true power. Lord Bô-Kedén has shown himself to you in your heart, as he has shown himself to me.

"But tremble in your heart, Baloe, as you hold the staff of the Allwise. For why has he chosen to show himself to you? Tremble with me upon this mountain. Bô-Kedén reveals his power to those such as we are, not as a fact only to be known. We are shown not only so we may speak of his will. As we know him in our hearts, we are his purpose in the world. Is the Center not within us as well? Tremble Baloe."

Many were the journeys that Baloe made to Mekloth. And as the years passed, so it was that the pupil became teacher as well. Each grew in wisdom and in friendship with the other. But while Mekloth remained on the mountain, Baloe returned always to Nebis. With staff in hand, he would teach the people of the words of Mekloth and of the Way of Bô-Kedén. And the people grew in spirit and in true wisdom.

-ABELA A' BALOHÉN-

THE EIGHTH PART

LATE SUMMER it was, and seven years after the Planting, Mekloth came down again to Nebis. With him rode one whose cloak was torn and stained with a dark red. And as they passed together through the town, the streets filled with cries of "Lerin! Lerin has returned! It is Lerin!" Many followed as Mekloth and the man made their way to the old house of Rakedén. There, Baloe met them at the east door, the door of greatest honor.

"Baloe, son of Rakedén, at last meet my old friend Lerin," Mekloth spoke, his arm about the man.

But Baloe sensed there was sadness in his voice. He embraced Mekloth's companion, saying, "Lerin of Baolind, welcome again to Nebis. Come into this house."

And as they entered, Baloe continued, "Lerin, what brings you this far east of Baolind so soon before harvest?"

Lerin halted. A great sorrow came across his face and he said, "Baolind is no more. This is the reason for my journey here." He walked to the window and looked out. "Nine days ago, Baolind was attacked by armies from the North. They left no house standing. They took no prisoners. It was all so sudden—many were killed.

"Timoth, the son of Kell, gathered an army to defend the town. I led a group to ruin bridges and destroy supplies, but the enemy was too strong. I have told Mekloth already that Timoth was killed in battle. My family is with those who escaped and fled to the South.

He turned to look at Baloe. "I knew I must travel to tell you this, for the Northerners will surely seek to avenge the loss here at Nebishan. You, Baloe, are in the greatest of danger. The head of the Son of Rakedén would bring a foot soldier much gold."

Baloe stood silent for a while before the two men, and then he spoke to Lerin, "How far are the Northerners from Nebis?"

"I cannot be sure. I fled Baolind to the South before coming here. Their armies could not have traveled far so soon after the battle, though. We were surprised and outnumbered, but the enemy lost much blood in taking our city. A three-day ride, maybe four."

"We must find out," Baloe said without hesitation.

He looked at Mekloth. "Will you travel toward Baolind with me? You know the Calan Plain as a soldier. As always, I need your help, and Nebis again depends upon it."

"It is nearly dark, Baloe," the Old One answered. "We should tell the people of the danger. Then we should prepare to depart tonight."

Lerin then spoke, "Feed my horse and provide me with supplies, and you will have two old soldiers riding with you."

"Good, then we three will leave tonight."

The people of Nebis were called together, and they were told of what had happened in the West. Mekloth told the plan to scout the enemy's position. And as all the townspeople listened, Baloe called out for them to seek their strength in Bô-Kedén, and to turn their minds to Him. Each then went to prepare in his way for the hardships that lay ahead.

As the sun set, the horses were fitted, and the final preparations were made. And all in Nebis was quiet as the three rode out toward the darkening western sky.

-THA ABELA-

THE NINTH PART

THE CALAN PLAIN is a land that lies between the wooded Calanite Mountains on its eastern and northern edge, and the rocky Western Range that bounds its opposite side. Many rivers and streams flow eastward across the gentle slope of the Plain, and eventually into the mighty Alban. Like a great arm, the River Alban wraps itself around the land, embracing the whole plain and nourishing its fields and towns. From its source in the high mountains of the northwest, it flows eastward, and then bending along the curve of the Calanite range, it surges southward past Nebis and on to the lowlands, where it finds its way to the sea. The way to Baolind took Mekloth, Lerin, and Baloe across the Great River Alban, then northward along her western shoreline. Soon they came to a large stream that flowed into the Alban from across the center of the plain, and the three turned to ride west toward Baolind. But they were careful to travel along the southern bank of the stream, for they could not be sure when they might come upon the enemy.

Through the night they rode, but at morning's first light, they crossed the stream at its fork and rode north and west, straight toward the town. Four days they rode, making camp along the way, and strange it happened that nowhere along the journey did they encounter the Northern armies. Then they were upon the town.

On the fifth day Lerin led them to the high ground outside Baolind. And as they neared the top of the rise, he stopped and held his hand out before him, saying, "Behold my beloved Baolind."

Below them lay the smoldering ruins of the town. Her buildings lay burned and broken. Her streets were filled with the rubble of defeat. The very air about the place tasted of death.

"The ones from the North have come to this place and have done this evil. They have taken a living city from us and have left it a lifeless ruin. And now they are gone. In the glory of victory, they have departed my Baolind. But this before you is their true glory, their true accomplishment. The victory of war is not carried from this place. It is forever mingled with the blood spilled on this soil, with the pain in the heart of the widow, with the tears of the children. This is their victory."

And Lerin bowed his head.

-THA ABELA LERENEI-

THE TENTH PART

AS THE THREE rode down to the ruined city, it was Mekloth who noticed the tracks leading to the North. But it was Baloe who first saw the smoke rising from the northern horizon.

"Look before us!" Baloe spoke. "Can another city be afire there?"

Mekloth raised himself high on his mount and stared intently at the great dark cloud of smoke rising in the distance.

He turned to Lerin. "Can it be Kelarus?"

Lerin shook his head. "Kelarus lies to the east of the fire. There are no cities or towns in that part of the Plain. He turned and looked gravely at Mekloth.

Mekloth spoke, "Then it is as before."

Lerin stared for a while at the smoldering horizon, then said with a guttural voice, "Long Scar...."

"What does this mean?" Baloe asked. "What is as before?"

"We will travel northward and you will see what has happened," Mekloth answered. And they set off, riding toward the great fire.

The ride was difficult, for along the way they encountered the last ranks of the enemy marching to the north. The three were forced to take the high trails and to avoid any conflict with the Northerners. As they neared the great fire, however, it became necessary to ride close to the enemy. But Baolind's misfortune proved good fortune for this journey, for the enemy soldiers and horsemen had more interest in carrying the plunder from the defeated city than desire to pursue some ragtag horsemen riding by. So the trip through the midst of the enemy was made without incident. The riders from Nebis rode across

31

the ranks of those from the North, until at last they made their way to a ridge above the roaring flames.

There they looked down upon the great fire. Clear to the river the forest was aflame, casting billows of angry smoke into the sky. The ground was blackened and littered with great fallen trees still burning. And down the rivershore from this, brilliant raging flames were leaping high alongside a stand of yet unburned trees. Only the marsh grass in the water escaped the searing destruction that fed itself upon all that grew green on the land.

Mekloth then spoke. "Baloe, we have seen the destruction of Baolind already. But this speaks the true desire of those who invade this plain. Look there to the shoreline where the fires are dying. Soldiers. They are casting the charred logs into the river where the strong currents of the Alban will carry them southward to Nebis. It is a message Long Scar sends to Nebis. The same message that was sent to us before Nebishan. He says to us that they will destroy the people of Bô-Kedén, the people who live according to the Wisdom of the Tree. They profane our faith and mock Lord Bô-Kedén by destroying this forest. They blacken the Alban with his blood. They boast that the Almighty falls before their might.

"It is as before. Nebis is what he seeks. The battle cannot be many days away."

Baloe was quiet as he looked out over the burning land, but Lerin spoke up angrily, "Why does Lord Bô-Kedén allow this to happen? They profane his name and burn the forests to spite him. Can he not smite them and take them from the face of the land? Why does the Almighty allow such evil to walk the earth?"

Mekloth answered him, "Our ways are not the Lord's ways. We follow Bô-Kedén and we seek to do good. But the Almighty does not do good as men do. His ways are not man's ways. The Lord does his will, while we do only good.

"But Lerin, the difficult part to understand is this," Mekloth continued. "As those from the North do evil, Bô-Kedén still works his will. His will is greater than their evil, as it is greater than the good we seek. No one can escape his Will, whether he does good or evil.

"The Will of mighty Keden moves all of history and creation. What man can finally know this Will and who can judge it? We cannot know how Bô-Kedén will use this great sacrilege through his great power, but we must remember that all events, good or bad, in the end do work the Lord's Will. They are not caused by the Lord, but they are the Lord's."

Then Lerin spoke again, "Mekloth, you are very wise in the way of Bô-Kedén, but I am just an old soldier. I cannot understand all you say. I cannot always understand the Way of this Lord. My city in ruins, this forest destroyed— I can only feel anger. But I am not angry at the Lord Bô-Kedén. My rage is against this enemy. I know that the Lord will prevail against them, and with my help."

"We shall need your help soon, it appears." It was Baloe who had spoken. "Do not turn about quickly, but cast your eyes down the slope behind us. We are being followed."

Far below them a band of enemy horsemen was crossing the creek that passed at the foot of the ridge toward their back. They were starting up the hill along the same path the riders from Nebis had taken. The lead rider was pointing out the trail the three had left. They were indeed being followed.

"Where shall we head, my two old soldier friends? The fire is before us, they are behind us."

Lerin spoke, "We should ride east to Kelarus. We will have to ride close to the fire, but we can manage. Perhaps the fire will burn over our trail."

Mekloth nodded. "Yes, we should ride to Kelarus. It is a safe place. But we should not elude the trackers. They must know we travel to Kelarus. Listen now: if they think we are from Nebis, they would have two choices—to kill us straight away or to follow us to our defenses. Since we are still very much alive, they must seek to know our positions. Let us ride—not too cautiously—to Kelarus. We may bluff the trackers into thinking that Nebis has sent assistance to the northern towns of the Plain. And we can surely advise the town of the enemy's intent."

Baloe nodded in agreement, and the three set off toward the east.

-THA ABELA-

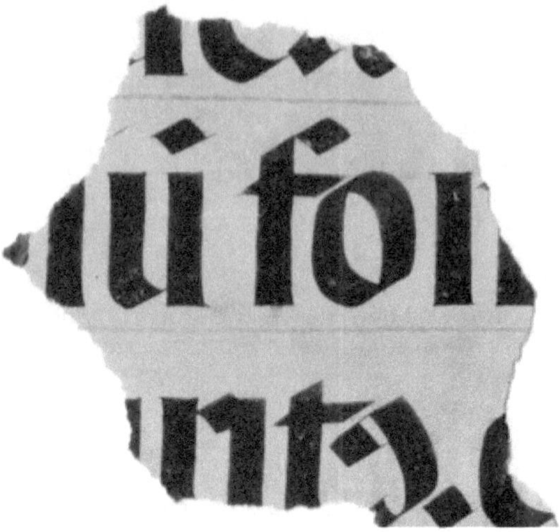

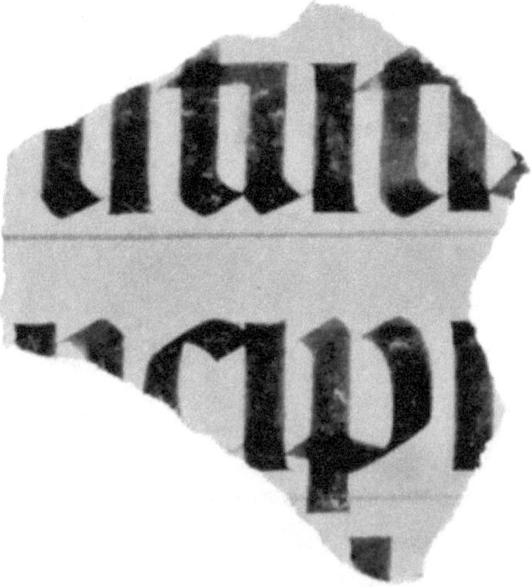

THE ELEVENTH PART

SHE KNEW they were coming. Before the fall of Baolind, she had seen them when she threw the salt into the fire. In the bluest flames she saw the riders, and she knew them. They would be troubled men with good hearts, men all brave. And they were knowers of the trees.

They would come to her, she knew. The oldest one would see to that, for he was keen. And in the blue flames she saw the youngest one would find her, for Bô-Kedén would lead him to the mound. The other one would also come, for he had no regard for danger in the midst of danger. Salt in the fire, he would come, too. Yes, from the forest they were coming to her.

✞✞✞

Beyond the oak forest of Koan, the riders urged their horses on, through the field of tangled vines and ivy. More than once the riders had to dismount to hack right and left through the knotted growth, or to free a horse's leg from the ivy's green tangle. It was as if the vines were knowing things, wanting to hold back these horses and these men, wanting to protect with briars what lay across the field. In time, the riders prevailed and were free of the pricking vines and binding cords of ivy. Wide before them lay a treeless place.

"Strange, there are no trees here," Lerin said. "And look there—" He rode ahead of the others and pointed downward. "These are ocean grasses."

Mekloth dismounted and ran his hand through long sea grass growing in a clump from the sandy soil. As his fingers combed the green blades, he looked around at what lay before them. His horse started to one side and pulled hard against the rein Mekloth held. The Old One calmed the restless horse and rubbed its nose. It licked his hand and grew calm again.

Lerin spoke. "Bô-Kedén must never have seen this place. In the middle of a Calan Forest—no trees. Sea grass growing all around, and we are a ten-day ride from the ocean. I say we leave this place the way we came. I prefer that affectionate ivy to this. Look at me—I'm sweating all over. Let's find us some Almighty shade." And Lerin turned his mount back toward the field of vines and the Koan Forest.

Mekloth remounted his horse, but it was still uneasy. It shuffled its hooves and edged sideways toward a white sandy path that led ahead through the sea grass. Mekloth reined in his mount and turned the horse around.

But Baloe did not follow.

As Lerin came to the place where the ivy grew thick, the youngest called out to Mekloth, "Teacher—this is strange. I am remembering the vision. The vision when we first met—"

Mekloth turned his horse about and rode back to Baloe. Lerin halted and looked over his shoulder at the others.

Baloe continued, "The vision of the trees and the seeds —"

"Yes, go on..." the Old One replied. His eyes revealed a deep sense of anticipation.

"The dead tree I saw —"

"Yes..."

Baloe turned and pointed across the field. "It is that tree. The tree in the distance beside the white hill there —"

On the far side of the wide sea of grasses stood a barren tree, majestic and dark beside a pure white rise of earth. The two features seemed joined in a perfect balance, each form different but somehow completing the other, the angular and skeletal reach of the great tree alongside the calm and comforting rise of the bright hill. They seemed ancient and eternal partners. And all about them the sea grasses waved in the breeze, like a beckoning gesture.

Lerin's horse ambled up beside the others. Mekloth's mount shook its head and snorted, as Mekloth gestured with his arm. "Lerin," the Old One spoke, "Across that field of sea grass is a tree we need to see."

Lerin turned to look at Baloe. The young man raised his eyebrows and nodded with a small smile. Lerin sighed. With sweat dripping from his hair and scruffy beard, he looked out over the parched field of waving grass, then back at Baloe. "We're going to see that tree. That tree over there... "

"Yes," Baloe replied.

"The dead one..."

"Yes."

"It couldn't be another dead tree, I guess..."

"No. It is that tree," Baloe replied.

"That tree," Lerin sighed.

"Yes," Mekloth said. "We need to see that tree."

Lerin looked back across the field of sea grass. "Well okay, then. Let's go and see what a dead tree has to say to us. I just hope we don't get any splinters in our ears..." At that he spurred his horse ahead, past Mekloth who was laughing. So it was that Lerin who had no regard for danger in the midst of danger, led the riders onto the white path and into the field of ocean grasses.

As they approached the great tree, less and less grass was growing alongside them. And beside the white hill, nothing grew at all. The hill sat purest white, glistening and surrounded by its small white desert that kept at bay all things green and growing. In the heat of the mid-day sun, the mound seemed smooth and cool, as if the moon were human and had fallen to earth. The shadow from its partner tree fell gently across its soft white surface, like a caring hand's touch.

"I know of this place," Mekloth said as a memory grew words. He dismounted. "Yes...I know this place." He walked to the edge of the mound. "Baloe, this is the Mound of Shâl-déh. I was told of this place years ago, but I did not think it was a real place. The Mound of Shâl-déh—Whitehill..."

Baloe had dismounted, and was walking, staff in hand, toward the tree.

Lerin was ready to leave and stayed on his mount. His horse lowered its head and ambled toward the white hill. Watching as Lerin's horse passed him,

Mekloth spoke to the animal, "So that's why you horses were restless. Lerin, let him go there. It is salt."

Lerin's horse moved ahead and, bowing low, began to lick the smooth surface of the Whitehill. And the other two horses soon followed their noses to the mound.

"The Mound of Shâl-déh? This is the Mound from the *Canticles*? We are there—here?" Lerin asked.

But the Old One did not reply straight away. In silence he scanned the contour of the mound and walked along its white edge before stopping. Then in a full voice Mekloth began to sing the old song:

> In the time before the Dreaming
> Before N'ka dreamed trees to being,
> Before the land was dry,
> Before the sky had brightened,
> In the Dawning time it was
> That Shâl-déh rose from earth,
> And rounded was her form.
> The deer came tame unto her,
> The hrelah and the Calan lion.
> All came low to Shâl-déh
> To nourish at her breast....

Then, as if from nowhere, a woman's voice rose to finish Mekloth's song:

> Sing we now the story of
> The Mound of Shâl-dekáh.

Startled by the voice, Baloe and Lerin stepped back, not knowing in this strange place who else it was that sang. Mekloth nodded deeply to the tall woman as she approached. She came toward the three with grace and knowing confidence. Her white cloak waved as she walked, like sea grasses in a gentle wind.

Then Mekloth spoke to her, "You are the Raíga of Whitehill."

"I am that," was her reply. "And more I am."

Mekloth then responded, "I am…"

"You are Mekloth," she spoke with authority, "Son of At-Kedén. He is remembered well for his wise council and his generosity."

Mekloth nodded low and spoke in the Old Tongue, "*Eanos 'an kaitaínos. Shâld-akanos al natah.*" And he touched his hand to his mouth.

The Keeper of the Mound replied in kind, "*At-kedenaís sha ehnakah hatón. Uios kedenoi gnos istimos atáh. Seh hatáh.*" Then she turned her face toward Baloe and Lerin who stood spellbound in the shadow of the great tree. She gestured for them to come to her, and said to them, "*Bô-Kedénaís tha yah Shâl-dekáh. Seh atáh.*"

The two could only bow low before her.

"Baloe," she spoke as she touched his face and looked deeply into his eyes, "Your faithfulness to your vision from Bô-Kedén has brought you here to me. It will also save your people. These things I know, this and more, as I am the Raíga of Shâl-dekáh. *Bián cumulaí âs gnos atáh.*" And she cast salt all about on the white ground before her.

"The Way of Shâl-dekáh is the hidden way. It stands beside Lord Bô-Kedén. One in truth, each completes the other."

As the Raíga spoke, a fox trotted up to the white hill and began licking salt beside the horses. "As Bô-Kedén draws all unto himself, so it is with Shâl-dekáh. The deepest life in human beings tastes of her grace. Her salt has touched both tears and blood. All rivers flow to oceans. They turn across the earth to find their ways to her white salt.

"The Wisdom of the Raíga is now spoken." She stepped into the black shadow of the tree. "An old seed will ride desire for Shâl-dekáh. And by this, a new seed will be delivered." She turned and looked directly at Baloe and said, "*Seh atáh. Seh atáh.*" And the Keeper of the Mound turned and threw salt upon the ground before the three. "Travel well," the Raíga said. She looked deliberately at each face, then bowed with ancient grace.

The men gathered their horses as the Raíga of Whitehill watched, smiling and in silence. As the three rode past the great tree its bare limbs and branches split the sunlight that fell across them, touching their skin as if its light were arms and hands that gave each a parting deep embrace.

The white path delivered the riders past the field of ocean grasses to the place of vines. As Lerin's horse struggled back down the ivy-tangled trail, the shaggy traveler turned around and spoke to his companions, "War is all around us, but I have to say, that Raíga—she was a beauty wasn't she? That elegant white dress and that youthful face with those jade-green eyes. That chestnut hair…reminds me of my wife when we first met —"

"Are your eyes failing, Lerin?" It was Mekloth who spoke with a laugh as he rode. "The Raíga's eyes were as blue as the heavens. And her hair was—was like purest silver. I wouldn't call her youthful, exactly. I'd say that hers was a timeless beauty." He paused and thought. "She reminded me of Baloe's mother a bit."

"Golden hair like summer sunlight streaming through the trees," Baloe said. "And her eyes—they were wide and brown. Like a fawn's eyes, I'd say —"

At once they all reined their horses to a stop and looked at one another. Even the horses in their silence seemed to know. They had met the Raíga at Whitehill, the Keeper of the Mound. But she was more than this. In that strange place they had been in the very presence of the Shâl-dekán Taon, the consort of Lord Bô-Kedén. It was Baloe who knew the lines from the *Canticles*, and spoke them straight away:

> Mirror of the heart, candle in the night,
> The hidden face of Shâl-dekáh is every man's delight.

Mekloth smiled and nodded slowly, for he knew that it was Baloe who would understand best what she had told them by the mound, and in the shadow of the great tree.

-THA ABELA AI SHALDE-KEI-

THE TWELFTH PART

ALONG THE RIVER they rode, and behind them the enemy followed. As darkness fell, the three made camp, keeping careful watch through the moonless night. At morning's first light they were off again toward Kelarus. A half-day ride east and they had come to the city.

Now Kelarus was the most ancient town on the Calan Plain. Though it was small in comparison to cities such as Nebis and Baolind, it had once been the most important place in the region. Hundreds of years before, the Old Dwellers of the Plain had built around the city a great stone wall that defended the place against all enemies. For ten generations the walls of Kelarus had kept the town safe, and her people had prospered.

As the riders from Nebis approached the town, they saw her gates were closed fast. Kelarus had already prepared for the enemy.

The three rode to the great gate and pounded hard at the window. After a wait that seemed too long there was a noise inside, and the wooden shutter was pulled open, partly at first, then completely and with a sharp crack.

The guard within spoke gruffly, "What is your business here?"

Lerin answered him, "We have ridden here to tell you of your enemy's positions. I am from Baolind and am called Lerin. My friends here, Mekloth and Baloe, ride from Nebis. We must enter and talk of an alliance between Kelarus and the towns to the south."

"And who are the ones on the hill who rode in behind you?" the guard asked.

The three turned and looked up the road behind them. At the edge of the forest the trackers had halted their mounts and were looking down upon the town.

Mekloth looked at Lerin, then spoke to the guard, "I believe they are Northern troops that have followed us here. They know we are from Nebis. It is important that they see us freely enter Kelarus. They will then believe that your town has been given assistance by Nebis. If we are turned away, they will know that Kelarus is alone in defending itself. For your own safety, you must let us enter."

"How can I know you, yourself, are not our enemy?" the guard grunted back.

"You must believe us," was Mekloth's only reply.

"Very well. You may enter. But your mounts must remain outside the walls. It is a military order that no strangers may enter the city with their mounts. You can tie up over there by that mule."

Mekloth spoke again, "We cannot do as you say. The Northerners who watch us must not suspect that we are strangers to you, or our coming here is all for nothing. They must see us welcomed, not as strangers leaving our stock outside the walls, but as Southern allies who have scouted their positions."

"I know what you are saying. Perhaps you are right," the guard answered back. "But I have my orders. No strangers may bring their stock into the town."

Baloe then spoke, "Sir, very well. We will come in. And to thank you for allowing us to escape our enemies, we give you our horses. We were the owners, but they are now yours."

Mekloth turned to Lerin, and concealing a smile, whispered under his breath, "He is indeed the son of Rakedén."

"I do not understand," the guard replied. And Lerin was just as confused.

"It is simple," Baloe said, grasping his staff firmly. "I wish to thank you for allowing us safe entry into your town. So I am making you a gift of our three horses. Please now, open the door so we may enter. And you may also allow the horses in, since they are not owned by strangers, but rather are owned by yourself."

A grin then shot across Lerin's face.

The guard was silent for a while, and then he spoke, "Very well. Either you are the cleverest three men to come to this gate, or you are the most foolish. I do not know which. Come to the gate and I will take you and the horses in—my horses, mind you."

"Your horses," Baloe nodded with a smile.

And so it was, the enemy saw the three enter Kelarus with the horses, and the trackers from the North returned to report what they had seen.

As night fell, Mekloth, Lerin, and Baloe told the people of Kelarus what they had seen and done, and the leaders were grateful upon hearing these things. All talked together of their common interest in resisting the ones from the North. But after the three had eaten and rested a while, they walked to the great gate and prepared to depart for Nebis.

As they readied for the return, they were joined by none other than the guard they had first met at the gate. He walked up to them with the travelers' horses in tow. Without looking any of the three men in the eyes, he spoke to them, "I have come to thank you for your journey here. I suppose I should also thank you for these horses, but I cannot help feeling that I have cheated you."

Baloe replied to him, "But you did not cheat us, Sir. It was my idea that the horses should be yours. You had your orders to follow, and we needed above all to enter through your gate with our mounts. All has turned out well."

"But now you must return to Nebis on foot," the guard responded. "It will take four days to make the journey, even if you start tonight."

Baloe again spoke, "So it may. But time was not the most important thing to consider here. It rarely is the most important thing. It was better that we chose to preserve life."

Then Mekloth placed his hand on Baloe's shoulder and said to the guard, "You see, it was a gamble. My young friend, here, bargained our three horses to you for the possibility that the enemy will not attack your city. If the

Northern troops do not attack this place, and there are no lives lost, then that is quite a purchase for three tired horses, wouldn't you say?"

The guard threw up his hands in exasperation, saying, "I've never seen men so happy to lose three fine mounts! You Tree People—I'll never understand you..."

Lerin then got in on it. "Let's face it. You and I are just simple fellows, and these two are much smarter than we are. They've got strange ways of getting things done, but they do get things done."

At that the guard began laughing, saying, "Ha! Imagine it! I came here to offer to give you back the horses, but I do believe he wouldn't take them —"

"You are right," Baloe replied. "The horses are yours. It was our bargain."

"Very well then," the guard grunted, at last looking at Baloe. "I have a small boat on the river." He stabbed the air with his finger, pointing toward the water, "It is yours. It's not much, but it will carry the three of you safely downriver to Nebis. You will be there in a day," the guard continued. "Take the boat, but please let's not talk about it. You make things much too complicated for me. Just take it. This much at least I can do for you. You'll find it tied to a post in the water at the end of the wide path to the river. It is the only boat you will see there."

"We thank you, Sir Guard," Lerin said with a slight bow. "But please do me one favor".

"What is it?"

"One favor is all I ask." Lerin said.

"Then ask it."

"Just a small favor it will be."

"Ask it, Man!" the exasperated guard blurted out. "Ask it!"

"It's about my horse, Melish," Lerin said as he scratched his horse's chestnut head.

"Yes, spit it out, Man. Spit it out..."

44

"Well…we were inseparable, and…."

"Yes—go on…"

"He likes hay every day," Lerin said, rubbing his horse's nose. "Every day but Sundays."

"Every day…but Sundays." The guard repeated, with waning patience.

"That's it. Every day but Sundays," he said with a wide smile and a quick nod of his shaggy head. "That's because on Sundays, Melish likes oats."

"Oats?"

"Right…oats on Sundays. That's the only favor I ask you. Would you give dear Melish his oats on Sundays?" Lerin said with his right eyebrow raised.

By this time Baloe was having to hold back his laughter. Mekloth had to turn away to hide a widening smile.

"And Melish likes his oats cooked…" At that all the men but Lerin broke out into loud hoots and guffaws.

"…And with a just little milk," Lerin said with utmost seriousness. "And the smallest dash of honey. That's all I ask. I love that horse."

So it was that after bidding farewell to the guard, the horses, and the others at Kelarus, the three set off into the black night, following the path to the river and to the boat.

-THA ABELA-

THE THIRTEENTH PART

THE THICK DARKNESS of the empty night sky hung heavy over the travelers as they made their way to the river. The moon's light again was hidden. Between Kelarus and the river the forest was strangely still. As the three continued on the worn path toward the river, Lerin suddenly stopped. Then he silently motioned the others to the ground as he moved quickly behind a tree.

There were voices. On the river's edge there were voices. It was a northern dialect. The enemy was on the shoreline before them. And—strange—there was another noise. Beyond the nighttime choir of frogs and crickets. A hissing noise, like someone or something taking a long, shallow, but deep breath. In the blackness of the night, though, nothing could be seen.

Lerin drew close to the ground and moved nearer to the others. He spoke in a bare whisper, "We cannot get to the boat. The enemy is there. What shall we do?"

There was no reply.

"Shall we try to get back to Kelarus?" he asked.

"No." It was Baloe who had spoken. "The Lord Bô-Kedén is with us here. He has shown me a way."

Baloe raised his staff and, holding it firmly, he whispered, "We must get to the river."

But Lerin answered back in more than a whisper, "We cannot get to the boat."

Mekloth quickly put his hand on Lerin's arm, and Lerin continued more quietly. "There are at least a dozen men between us and the boat." His eyes were fixed with great urgency upon the young man.

But Baloe, as he tied a lashing to his staff, spoke again in a quiet but confident voice, "The Lord Bô-Kedén has shown me a way."

Then at once there were voices in the darkness behind them. Enemy voices.

Baloe quickly whispered, "Keep low. Follow me."

He led them off the path to the right, and then through the underbrush toward the river. They stopped. Then again they moved, through the grasses this time to the edge of the sandy riverbank. The voices were very close. And the strange, low hissing noise filled the black night air—not louder so much as larger.

Baloe looked out before them, then turned back to his companions. "Walk behind me," he whispered. "Across the beach to the river. After we wade past the shallows, swim hard to deep water."

"But we can't swim to Nebis —" Lerin said sharply.

Mekloth then spoke in a whisper, "Perhaps, Lerin, the Lord Bô-Kedén has shown him a way."

But Lerin had no time to reply, for Baloe straightaway stood, saying, "Follow me," and he slung his staff across his shoulder as he started across the sand. Mekloth at once was behind him, and Lerin followed.

The three were knee-deep in the river before the enemy realized their presence. There was then a great commotion on the riverbank. But even as torches were lit and held high along the shoreline, the three from Nebis were swimming hard in the deep waters of the Alban.

"Is it too soon to ask —" Lerin sputtered between strokes, "What do we do now?"

Baloe stopped swimming, and as he measured his strokes to keep afloat he answered, "Swim until you touch something—something firm in the water…careful not to burn yourself —"

"A bad joke Baloe —" was Lerin's sharp reply.

"This is no joke I think —" It was Mekloth who spoke. "The trees from upriver—the great fire, Lerin…."

"Yes," Baloe continued as the water lapped against his staff. "The hissing—some wood is still hot—cover the tree with your cloak…. River Alban will carry us—and the logs to Nebis."

And at those words, the river surged, speeding the three southward as they began to swim to the heart of the river. As the river current carried Lerin ahead of the others, he called back over his shoulder excitedly, as he continued slapping at the water, "The Lord has—shown you a way indeed! But let's find these hot trees—before I drown!"

Soon each had found a charred trunk that would hold a man. And as all on the river hissed about them on that dark night, the three from Nebis held tight to blackened bark. By morning the swift waters of the Alban had carried them well into the South.

The burned forests of the North,

the great sacrilege against Bô-Kedén

had become their way

home.

-ABELA-

THE FOURTEENTH PART

THE SUN was well into the morning sky when Mekloth called to the others. "We need to go ashore. We are not far from Nebis, and we need to talk with each other about the enemy. The people of Nebis will look to us as their leaders. We must know our minds about what we have seen and what we should prepare to do. We must know the Will of Bô-Kedén in all of this."

Lerin and Baloe agreed, and each made his way to the riverbank. There they gathered wood in silence and built a fire. It was done according to the oldest custom. Each man took two pieces of wood, one in each hand, and held them high into the air, as if human arms became wooden branches reaching skyward. The old words were spoken, and the first wood was positioned in a circle. Then more wood was stacked in a smaller circle atop this round base. Small kindling twigs were placed inside the arrangement so that the smallest branches pointed upward, as if they were growing. A green leafy branch was placed in the center, and the youngest lit the fire. It was a fire to honor Lord Bô-Kedén and the power of His deliverance. Seated about the fire the men talked together of the strength of Nebis and of the threat of the enemy. They spoke of plans to defend and to attack, of preparations to be made, and of allies to seek out. The fire burned hot to glowing coals as they talked.

Then Baloe poked the embers with his staff, and as a shower of sparks rose, he spoke, "We must make battle with the enemy according to the plans we make here. We may overcome the enemy. But if victory will be ours, it will be because of the Will of Lord Bô-Kedén, just as it was at Nebishan."

Mekloth nodded. "You are right in this. We fool ourselves if we rely on our own power. We must first know the Lord's Will."

It was then Lerin's turn to speak. "His Will is surely to resist his enemies. Can it be anything but this? But how shall we do this? The Lord's Will is so difficult to know. The sacred Word given in the past has so much truth, but what does it mean for us now? The *Canticles* and *Sayings* do not tell us how to win this war."

Baloe's reply was calm as he stared into the fire. "Lord Bô-Kedén has given his Word in the past. He will give it to his people again. He is with his people always, even as he was with us in the night outside of Kelarus. We must only be ready to listen."

At those words, Baloe reached into his shirt and drew out a leather pouch. He placed it on the sand before him and turned toward Mekloth. The Old One looked deep into the young man's eyes, and for a long while there was only the sound of the crackling fire.

Then Mekloth spoke softly to Baloe, "I heard her words at Whitehill. She said them to you: 'An old seed will ride desire for Shâl-dekáh. And by this, a new seed will be delivered.' But it is for you to decide. It is the Way of the Planting. Only you will know how it should be done, and when."

Once more there was silence about the fire. Then Baloe reached and took up the pouch. And opening it he shook a seed into his hand, saying, "*Kaeres es. Kaeres es.* Again, it is time to Plant the Bô-Kedén."

And he took his staff and laid it beside him. And closing his eyes he brought the seed to his mouth, and at once fell into a dream.

-EYASKAN NEVESIN-

THE FIFTEENTH PART

UPON AWAKENING Baloe said this, "Mekloth, Lerin, this is my dream:

"I dreamt that Lord Bô-Kedén had called me to travel to him, for he desired to give counsel to those who believed in him. So I gathered my leather shield and helmet, my bow and quiver, and my sword and scabbard to serve as my protection should I meet some enemy. And I set off on foot to meet Lord Bô-Kedén at an appointed place.

"My way took me through a forest that caused me much difficulty, for the trees grew very close together. So close did they grow alongside each other that in order to pass between them, I was forced to strip myself of my weapons, one by one. First, I left behind my shield, then my bow and quiver. As I came upon trees growing still closer together, I was forced to leave behind my helmet, my scabbard—which was Rakedén's before me—and finally I dropped my sword. And I continued on my way to receive the Word from Bô-Kedén our Lord.

"Presently I came to an open meadow encircled by trees. I knew that the way to Bô-Kedén was across this field, so I set off for the other side.

"As I walked, I noticed a young man walking toward me from the opposite side of the meadow. Coming closer to him, I could see that he was not just another man my age, for I could now see his face. To my surprise he looked like my own reflection in a dark pool. My eyes, my face, my hair, my build were all his. Or should I say his were all mine? We were exactly alike in every way but one. In his hand he held a drawn sword that glinted in the sunlight as he walked across the meadow toward me.

"Now having no weapon or protection, myself, I approached him warily as we both neared the center of the field. We stopped and stood, each facing the other. And I spoke first. I said, 'My name is Baloe, Son of Rakedén, from the town of Nebis. I must cross this field to meet with Lord Bô-Kedén, for He has called me to hear his Word.

"The Other then spoke these strange words, like a dark echo, 'My name is Baloe, Son of Rakedén, from the town of Nebis. My master has instructed me not to let you pass this way, and to kill you if I can.' And he readied his sword to strike me.

"Men of Nebis, I looked into his face and trembled before him, for it was my own face. And it was my own hand about to slay me.

"Only then did I lift my face and raise my arms to Lord Bô-Kedén. My prayer was true and my heart was set on peace. I could feel the power of Tree Bô-Kedén, the Mighty Keden, growing deep within me. My heart was never stronger than in that moment when I was touched by the wisdom and love of Bô-Kedén.

"And then it was that I realized that high above me I held a sword in my hand. As I stepped back and prepared to defend myself, I looked again toward the place where my enemy had been. There was no one to be seen. I was alone there in the field. The sword in my hand glinted in the sunlight.

"Was I the one or other in that field? I felt at times as both, but who I was I cannot say for sure. I only know that, alone in the field, I chose to throw the sword I held upon the ground. And I spoke aloud these words, 'I will go to receive the Word from Bô-Kedén my Lord.'

"Then I heard a voice speaking, as if it came clearly and quietly from every tree surrounding the meadow. And the voice was saying this: 'Here you have seen my Word for you.'

"And I awoke."

There was silence about the fire as the three men pondered the dream. It was Lerin who first spoke. "What can this mean for us? We must at all times find power in Bô-Kedén, as you did in your dream, and as we have done in the past. Can this be all that the Lord has told us?"

He turned to Mekloth who had listened in silence to what had been said. As the Old One gazed into the fire, he replied to Lerin, "It is true that in the past we have lived by trusting in the power of Bô-Kedén. If this is again the message our Lord sends us in the dream, I would say that we cannot be told of this too often."

Lerin spoke again. "Of course you are right. My tongue was again too hasty. But I had only hoped for some new Word from Bô-Kedén."

"I feel there is a new Word in this dream, a great Word from the Lord," Mekloth replied. "But I would first hear from Baloe who surely understands this dream best. A dream is first for the dreamer."

"My dream does speak a new Word," Baloe began, "and three times the Word was given. Listen: in the dream what happened on my way to Bô-Kedén is the Lord's Word to us. It is the counsel to those who believe in Him. It tells the way we must resist those who come again from the North."

"Then tell the new Word to me," Lerin spoke, leaning forward with anticipation.

Mekloth remained quiet but turned to hear Baloe speak.

"In the dream I believed myself to be on the way to receive wisdom from the Lord himself. But what I experienced on the way was the real Word. It told the Way of Bô-Kedén. So it is in our life as well. Bô-Kedén speaks to us at every moment, not only through the *Sayings* and the *Canticles*.

"In the dream there are three swords. It was because of the trees that I cast down the first sword in order to find my way to Bô-Kedén. But remember that these very trees later spoke to me as our Lord himself. The second was the blade of an enemy, but my enemy was one like myself. I turned to Bô-Kedén, and by his power that sword was gone, and the enemy was no more. The third sword I held in my hand, but I cast it aside speaking my intention to receive the Word of the Lord Bô-Kedén. Then it was then that the Lord spoke, saying, 'Here you have seen my word for you.'

"The new Word was spoken to us three times." As Baloe spoke, a breeze called up tongues of bright fire. "The new Word is this: we must put aside the swords. Even now we are called to continue in the Way of Peace. If we are enemies of those like us, we are first enemies of ourselves. The sword is only in the way of those who seek Bô-Kedén; it is not of the Way of Bô-Kedén. This is the counsel given to those who believe."

Having heard this, Lerin fell to his knees in the sand. Mekloth rose and raised his arms above him. He lifted his face to the branches above, saying: "*Bô-Kedén eyaskamos vos tiamos*. We have heard your word again." And he began to sing the ancient hymn *Dakamos*, and the others joined him:

> We praise the root that splits the rock,
> The trunk that fire and ice withstands,
> The shoots that lead us to the light,
> The seeds we hold within our hands.
>
> Your arms protect us from the wind,
> A thousand birds sing your delight,
> Your fingers from the sun defend,
> Your body turns our darkness bright.
>
> We with legs that grow like roots,
> And arms that spread as holy limbs,
> We who move are drawn to wonder
> As the lightning draws the thunder.
>
> Would we knew why we were made as you.

A deep silence fell across the river and the trees along the shore. Then a sudden wind blew from across the water and gave a rustling voice to the beech trees along the shoreline. And a noise from upriver turned Lerin's head.

"Horses? Look there —" he cried out as he pointed to the nearby shore. "It's three horses!" His words became laughter. "Ha! Would you look at that! Now don't those three fine horses look familiar?" He whistled a raucous note through his teeth and called out, "Here boy—here, Melish! Come on to me, you good horse, you!"

Mekloth grew a wide smile and gave Lerin a hearty clout on the shoulder. Baloe saw the blessing, but quickly turned his thoughts to another place. He looked down and poked the dying embers with his staff. A lick of flame arose as a spray of sparks skittered up into the blue morning sky.

-THA ABELA-

THE SIXTEENTH PART

SO NOW the three made their way to Nebis, bearing the new Word of Lord Bô-Kedén. Once there, they called the town together and told all of what they had seen. They spoke of the Northern Enemy, of Baolind in ruins, of the Great Unholy Fire. They told of the strangeness of Whitehill, of their journey to Kelarus, and of their escape by night upon the River Alban. And the people listened as the three told of the Second Planting, and of the dream that spoke the new Word to those who would believe.

Then it was that the people called upon Baloe, Son of Rakedén, for they knew the Wisdom of the Lord was upon him. And they asked him to tell them how they should meet the enemy without weapons. And they listened to his words, for it was the Word of Bô-Kedén.

"O people of Nebis! Kedén calls us to cast aside the Way of Death. He calls us to a Way of Life which is before us now. We are called to put away the swords of war forever. But as we would not take the life even of an enemy, so we will not needlessly waste our own lives. For we must forever carry the Lord's wisdom so that all will know his way. The new Word is this, however: if we kill others to keep this wisdom, then we have already lost it.

"How then shall we continue to carry the Lord's wisdom? How shall we cast aside our swords and live? What is the way for us now?"

Baloe paused as he looked toward windblown trees moving in the distance.

✠✠✠

The morning air was thick with smoke. Tzokan leaned forward in his saddle and looked to the south toward Nebis. The long scar on his face burned a dark red. He slapped his restless stallion, and his armies responded, crying out loud as if theirs was one coarse voice. Their shout echoed back from the wall of oak forest that stood before them. Then all the Army of the North began to trudge southward toward battle, toward bloodshed, toward Nebis.

✠✠✠

The salt mound lay bright in the clear morning sun. The sea grass at Shâl-déh tossed itself about in the early breeze in an almost knowing way. Alone and elegant, the Raíga of Whitehill stood close by the great tree, her right hand gentle on it. Then she began to sing. The Shâl-dekán Taon began to sing.

✠✠✠

Baloe held out his arm and pointed toward the old ruins of Nebishan. "In times past we fought the enemy on the battle plains. We defended our lives, our possessions, our families, our faith. The victory was ours. But now the fields of combat have changed for us, the People of the Tree. The most important battle is now being waged in the heart. It is there that we risk our most important possession—the wisdom and power and love we are given through Bô-Kedén. It is only in the heart that the Way of Death will finally be defeated. The victory must again be ours.

"Listen: in the earth, as the root grows toward water, it takes the easiest path. But understand this—in growing, it does not take the easiest path only. It takes the easiest path to water. The easy way the root takes is a way to a thing most difficult to attain.

"We must become a people like roots in the soil, striving for a thing most difficult to attain. To be People of Bô-Kedén, we must now no longer be only the people of Nebis. We must rise up now and leave this place, each family its own way. We must grow to new towns, to new valleys. This is the way we will seek Bô-Kedén who is our water."

✠✠✠

Tzokan Long Scar jerked the reins hard to turn his mount. The startled horse winced and stumbled off the path over a fallen branch. The river at the broad ford before them was swollen with rain from the west. An old beech tree was down on the bank, blocking access to the shallows. Another was half-submerged in the water, its white limbs protruding from the muddy torrent.

60

Tzokan cursed. He lashed out at those around him, "Clear my way to Nebis. Hack this damned wood apart and burn it." Then with one sudden move he drew his sword and pointed it at the men. "Do it now or feel my blade. We ride south at daybreak."

✠✠✠

She was singing the First Songs, the songs of the Beginning. Beside the tree she walked through shadow and through light, her eyes half-closed. She moved with the beauty of sea grasses in soft wind, slowly turning as she sang, holding out her slender hands with grace, addressing earth's horizon with her gesture. The birds around were silent as she sang, as if they somehow recognized the old language and her solemn melody.

✠✠✠

Baloe looked out at the people, at the faces in the crowd. His mother. His sister and her child. And there was Mekloth, standing by an oak but somehow distant, his eyes part-closed in thought. Lerin stood beside him, head bowed. Baloe raised up his staff, and all the people gathered there fell silent, for they knew it was the staff of First Planting.

"People of Nebis: we will scatter across the land, but we will not die. The Power of Bô-Kedén will prevail. We will go to live among others, but the People of Bô-Kedén will not die. We will become the people, and they shall become the Lord's. Like green shoots we will grow out from this place to transform the Lord's earth. *Tha abela Taeon.*

"And now I say to you: after we have parted from this place like windblown seeds, we must remember to tell the children. Tell them in years to come of the Word of Bô-Kedén. And they must tell their children. We all will find new languages. A day may come when the name of Bô-Kedén will not be spoken. But the Word will still be told. Bô-Kedén will have new names. He will endure. We will learn the Lord has always had a thousand names. And we will know that Bô-Kedén is present with us always, as from the beginning. His wisdom is eternal, His power is boundless, and His love draws all unto himself. *Tha abela Taeon Nebishanah.*"

The new seed was delivered, as the Raíga had foretold and as Rakedén was shown at Nebishan. And now the seed was planted. The people of Nebis talked among themselves, considering what was spoken. Though a few chose to remain, the others readied themselves to depart the city. Within three days all who would leave the town had set off to find a new life, carrying with them the new Word of Bô-Kedén. By this the nations were planted.

Lerin traveled south by west, finding his family in the village once called Delan. Mekloth set out toward the north for the place called Whitehill. It is said that Baloe, staff in hand, led his family eastward, crossing the mountains into Cestium. Though others say there was a wise Old One called Balo-Kedénis who lived on the great island that lies before the mouth of the River Arnat.

Tzokan's fate was strange. A madness came upon him as he camped beside the Alban. A singing came into his tent and woke him in the night. It took his sleep away and left him with a growing rage. It was a song that only he would hear. Through the nights, persistent as the moon, it chafed against his mind. His soldiers once saw him bellow and slash his tent, as if canvas were the enemy. He stumbled from his shelter, bleeding, as in his private battle he had cut himself.

And this is what they say: his final night they found Tzokan walking in the woods and sweating from a fever. They say that he was singing, but no one understood the song.

Thus it is written.

And thus it was told to me

by one who showed me an ancient leather pouch.

In it there was a seed.

WRATTOR A-KAELON THOE SCRATOTH.

✠✠✠

Remnants

In the midway of our mortal life,
I found me in a gloomy wood, astray
Gone from the path direct: and e'en to tell
It were no easy task, how savage wild
That forest, how robust and rough its growth,
Which to remember only, my dismay
Renews, in bitterness not far from death.

Dante, *Inferno, Canto I*

In the Golden Legend we read that Adam, during his last illness, sent his
son Seth...to ask the Archangel Michael to send him the Oil of Mercy
which had been promised him at the time of his expulsion from Eden.
But instead of this the Archangel gave Seth some seeds which, if placed
beneath the tongue of the Progenitor of mankind and buried with him,
would take root and produce a tree from the wood of which would
eventually be made the Cross, the pledge of mercy for all mankind.

Enzo Carli, *Piero Della Francesca*

The *Tlalocan*-bound dead were not cremated as was standard custom, but
instead were buried in the earth with seeds planted in their faces and blue
paint covering their foreheads. Their bodies were dressed in paper and
accompanied by a planting stick put in their hands.

Archaeological description of Aztec religious practice

The sacred itself is plainly a mystery of consciousness, using the word
mystery to signify not a problem that can be intellectually solved, but a
process of awakening and transformation that must be acted out in order

to be experienced, and experienced if one is to make it one's own. Its taste is at once sweet and bitter, for it deals continually with both sides of a question in order to arrive at a position that can contain them both.

Francis Huxley, *The Way of the Sacred*

Is the laurel of triumph made of leaves or corpses? Is it adorned with ribbons, or with tombs? Is it bedewed with ointments, or with the tears of wives and mothers?

Tertullian, *De Corona*

And he said, So is the Kingdom of God, as if a man should cast seed into the ground; And should sleep, and rise night and day, and the seed should spring and grow up, he knoweth not how. For the earth bringeth forth fruit of herself, first the blade, then the ear, after that the full corn in the ear. But when the fruit is brought forth, immediately he putteth in the sickle, because the harvest is come.

The Gospel of Mark, 4:26-29 (The Version of King James)

You will not sleep, if you lie there a thousand years, until you have opened your hand and yielded that which is not yours to give or to withhold. You may think you are dead, but it will only be a dream; you may think you have come awake, but it will still be only a dream. Open your hand, and you will sleep indeed—then wake indeed.

George MacDonald, *Lilith*

The religious person is the one who believes that life is about making some kind of journey. The non-religious person is the one who believes there is no journey to take.

Monica Furlong, *Traveling In*

Furthermore, we have not even to risk the adventure alone, for the heroes of all time have gone before us. The labyrinth is thoroughly known. We have only to follow the thread of the hero path, and where we had thought to find an abomination, we shall find a god. And where we had thought to slay another, we shall slay ourselves. Where we had thought to travel outward, we will come to the center of our own existence. And where we had thought to be alone, we will be with all the world.

Joseph Campbell, *The Hero with a Thousand Faces*

But it is the silence, the waitingness of the place, that is so haunting; a quality all woods will have on occasion, but which is overwhelming here—a drama, but of a time-span humanity cannot conceive. A pastness, a presentness, a skill with tense the writer in me knows he will never know; partly out of his own inadequacies, partly because there are tenses human language has yet to invent.

John Fowles, *The Tree*.

For more than a month, Siddhartha meditated beneath a fig tree. After seven weeks, he rose, thanked the tree for providing shade, and immediately found Enlightenment. It was then that he became The Buddha, or The Enlightened One. Just as Siddhartha became the Buddha, the tree became the Bo Tree, the Tree of Enlightenment. Cuttings were taken from the original Tree, and these were propagated in many places.

An account of the Bodhi Tree

The old writings tell of the Gaelic belief in sacred trees. Such trees were spoken of as "*bile*" (BY-luh) in early texts, and they were associated with Royal Inauguration sites. The *bile* stood as symbols of kingships and ruling dynasties, and their destruction was the goal of a king's enemies. In 981, when the King of Meath and his men sought to attack Brian Boru (Brian Bóruma mac Cennétig), they went straight away to Maigh Adhair, the inauguration site of Brian Boru's clan the Dal Cais. The attacking army cut down the sacred *bile* there and dug up its roots. But the tree would not die. We read, as well, that in 1099 Domhnall Ua

Lochlainn of the northern Uí Néill defeated the Ulster men and completed the defeat by cutting down their sacred tree, the Craebh-Tulcha. The men of Ulster exacted revenge in 1111 by destroying the sacred grove of trees at the inauguration site of the Uí Néill. And likewise, in 1129 enemies of the Kings of south Galway cut down their red birch *bile*. The sacred trees of Ireland were rooted in blood-soaked earth.

Extracted from the *Irish Annals*

A grove there was, untouched by men's hands from ancient times, whose interlacing boughs enclosed a space of darkness and cold shade, and banished the sunlight far above...gods were worshiped there....no wind ever bore down on that wood, nor thunderbolt hurled down from the black clouds; the trees, even when they spread their leaves to no breeze, rustled of themselves... The people never resorted there to worship at close quarters but left the place to the gods.

This grove was sentenced by Caesar to fall before the stroke of the axe...But strong arms faltered; and the men, awed by the solemnity and terror of the place, believed that, if they aimed a blow at the sacred trunks, their axes would rebound against their own limbs.

Lucan, Roman poet, *Pharsalia*, Book III

The Lithuanians were not converted to Christianity till towards the close of the fourteenth century, and amongst them at the date of their conversion the worship of trees was prominent. Some of them revered remarkable oaks and other great shady trees, from which they received oracular responses. Some maintained holy groves about their villages or houses, where even to break a twig would have been a sin. They thought that he who cut a bough in such a grove either died suddenly or was crippled in one of his limbs.

James Frazer, *The Golden Bough, chapter IX*, "The Worship of Trees"

Experto crede: aliquid amplius invenies in silvis, quam in libris.
Trust the one who has experience: you will find something far greater in the woods than in books.

Bernard of Clairvaux, letter to H. Murdac

Psithurism, then, is a noun used to describe the sound of rustling leaves. It is, apparently, an adaptation of the Ancient Greek ψιθύρισμα (psithurisma) or ψιθυρισμός (psithurismos), which are derived from ψιθυρίζω (psithurizō, meaning 'I whisper').

Sconzani, "Wild Words"

✝✝✝

Old Nebishan Language, Words, and Phrases

in the *Planting of Bô-Kedén*

Arbolas vibayos! (4)
The tree lives!

Kaeres es. (5, 9, 11, 52)
It is the time.

Abela (5, 13, 18, 20, 49)
It is said

Mekloth ek baen. (8, 18)
I am Mekloth.

Tha Abela Makloht (21)
Thus said by Mekloth (Honorific Mode†)

Abela A' Balohen (26)
It is said unto Baloe

Tha Abela (28, 33, 45, 57)
Thus it is said

Tha Abela Lerenei (30)
Thus Lerin said (Lerin said this)

Mekloth to Raiga:
Eanos 'an kaitaínos. Shâld-akanos al natah. (39)
We are under a blessing. Priestess of Shaldakan, greetings. (Literally Priestess of Shaldakan we are "born of you" or "we are relatives.")

Raiga responds to Mekloth:
At-kedenaís sha ehnakah hatón. (39)
At-Keden had (Past Ringing Tense*: had and continues to have) true wisdom.

Uios kedenoi gnos istimos atáh. (39)
(His) son keeps now (Present Ringing Tense*) the knowledge of Keden (Bô-Kedén).

Seh hatáh. (39)
I say (it) now. (Intensified form of "now," and Present Ringing Tense* of say)

Raiga to Baloe and Lerin:
Bô-Kedénaís tha yah Shâl-dekáh. (39)
Multiple meanings:
You men of Bô-Kedén, I am (permanent form, first person) Shâl-déh.
You men of Bô-Kedén, I am (permanent form, first person) of Shâl-déh (deity).
You men of Bô-Kedén, I am (permanent form, first person) of Shâl-déh (place).

Seh atáh. (39)
I say (it) now (Present Ringing Tense*).

Raiga to Baloe:
Bián cumulaí âs gnos atáh. (39)
The knowing builds/grows well now (Present Ringing Tense*).

Seh atáh. Seh atáh. (39)
I say it now. I say it now (Present Ringing Tense*).

Tha abela ai Shalde-Kei (40)
Thus it was said at Shâl-dekáh.

Tha abela Taeon. (61)
Thus says the Lord.

Tha abela Taeon Nebishanah. (61)
Thus says the Lord of Nebis.

† Old Nebishan has vestiges of a still older form of the language. These older forms are found in certain ceremonial language contexts and when persons of high regard are addressed. This mode of expression, known to us as the Honorific Mode, was understood by its audience as an archaic form of speech that gave the content special gravitas and power. It extended the highest respect to persons thus addressed. This mode of address and speech involved a reversion to older forms of noun cases and verb conjugation.

* Old Nebishan Language verbs in the "Ringing Tense," past or present, have a time component to their meanings that conveys ongoing action or persistence, likened to the continuing sound of a struck bell. The verb continues to act permanently into the future. These "Ringing Tenses" are somewhat comparable to "progressive" and "continuous" tenses in later European languages.

Translator's Note: Several elements of the language of "The Eleventh Part" of the *Planting of Bô-Kedén* have an affinity with language we find in the fragments of the *Sayings* that are preserved in Carew Manuscripts 17 and 23. In particular, we note in both the *Sayings* and the Raíga section of the *Planting* the frequent use of the word "*atáh*" (translated in English as "now") in contexts we might describe as prophetic. The frequent use of the "Ringing Tense" is a related characteristic shared by both the *Sayings* fragments and the "The Eleventh Part." In addition, there are in both manuscript portions the somewhat surprising references to salt and its ceremonial use. For those reasons, and given the very early date now assigned to the *Sayings*, some scholars (Richardson, 2014; Damico, 2018; Seth-Iversen, 2019) have argued that "The Eleventh Part" may derive from a source that was written considerably earlier than the *Planting of Bô-Kedén* manuscript compiled by the author we know as the "Writer of Calan." Seth-Iversen argues further that the fire-building portion of the "Fourteenth Part" derives from the *Sayings*, as well. The recent discovery in the Vatican Archives of "new" leaves of a *Sayings* manuscript may shed light on these interpretations.

www.ingramcontent.com/pod-product-compliance
Lightning Source LLC
Chambersburg PA
CBHW031859170626
46807CB00004B/1798